Look up into the sky. Can you see the rainbow? It arches like a bridge over the hills and comes down into Nutshell Wood. At the end of the rainbow, deep in the wood, a tiny magical village is appearing. That village is Rainbow's End. Rainbow's End can only be seen by humans when a rainbow is in the sky, otherwise it is invisible to everyone except the gnomes who live there and the woodland animals.

The gnomes of Rainbow's End are jolly little folk who are always busy. Lots of exciting and interesting things happen in the village and no one is ever bored. This book tells the story of something that happened there. A little bird told me!

Rainbow's End
TODDY AND THE FOX
Written & Illustrated by John Patience

PUBLISHED BY PETER HADDOCK LIMITED
BRIDLINGTON, ENGLAND

Toddy Meadows and Tiny Toadflax were on their way to move a tree which had been blown down in the previous night's storm and was blocking the main road through Rainbow's End. Suddenly, a stone flew past Toddy's nose and hit a dandelion clock, sending the seeds flying up into the air. Pip had fired the stone from his catapult. "Sorry, Mr Meadows," he said. "I didn't see you coming." "That's all right," replied Toddy, patting Pip's head. "No harm done." As Toddy went on his way he began thinking about the catapult. He was a very inventive gnome and Pip's toy had given him an idea. "Yes, I'll have to work on that," he muttered.

The fallen tree was much too big for the gnomes to
drag away, so Toddy decided that if they made two
saw cuts through it, then they could simply move the
section which was blocking the road. The two gnomes
were hard at work when Tiny heard a rustling sound
in the long grass near by and glimpsed two sharp
eyes, two pointed ears and a long red muzzle. "It's a
fox!" he cried. "Run for your life." Foxes are the
only animals in the woods which the gnomes are
afraid of, and Toddy and Tiny dropped the saw and
ran like the wind!

With the fox close on their heels, the gnomes scampered up a tree. The fox leapt up but only managed to tear the seat of Tiny's trousers. This made them both very angry; Tiny because they were new trousers and the fox because he had narrowly missed a tasty lunch. He prowled around the foot of the tree for some time before at last giving up and going off in search of easier prey. "Phew! That was a close thing!" exclaimed Tiny, examining his trousers. "Yes," agreed Toddy, "Let's hope we won't be seeing any more of him."

Later that day Hazel Hornbeam was picking bluebells for her mother when she began to get the feeling that someone was watching her. Glancing nervously over her shoulder she saw the fox. Hazel gave a startled cry and rushed off down the woodland path, with the fox close behind her. Suddenly, she tripped and fell head over heels down a dark hole. She landed on something soft which gave a grunt of surprise. It was a friendly old badger.

Hazel explained what had happened and the badger,
who was always a very helpful animal, decided that he
had better take her home himself, just in case the fox
should reappear. It was dusk by the time the badger
and Hazel reached the Hornbeam house. Mr and Mrs
Hornbeam had been very worried about Hazel and
were naturally most grateful to the badger for escort-
ing her home. They invited the kind old animal in for
a bite to eat, but like all badgers he was really rather
shy and, shaking his head, he mumbled his goodbyes
and disappeared into the night.

The fox continued to be a problem, lurking in the woods around the village and many of the gnomes could tell of close escapes from him. Sooner or later,

if nothing was done to get rid of him, one of the gnomes, perhaps a little one or an old one who couldn't run very fast, would be caught! It was decided that a meeting should be held in the village hall, which was really a great hollow oak tree. Dewy Hornbeam chaired the meeting and, calling it to order, he said gravely, "Now you all know why we are here. Does anyone have an idea how we can get rid of this fearsome fox?" There was a long silence. Then Toddy Meadows stood up and said mysteriously, "Just leave it to me. I think I have the solution."

The next day Toddy and Tiny were busy in their workshop. The gnomes passing by could hear the sound of their hammering and sawing. "It must be something to do with Toddy's plan," they told each other. Eventually Toddy and Tiny appeared in the village square, pulling a weird contraption behind them. It would be difficult for me to describe it. I had better say that it looked exactly as it does in this picture. "What is it?" everyone asked. "It's a giant catapult," replied Toddy.

The device was pulled to the edge of the village and, under Toddy's instructions, loaded with bags of flour. Now Billy Hornblower was told to blow his horn. The sound echoed through the trees and shortly, who should appear but Mr Fox. Everyone except Billy was well hidden and the fox, seeing only one defenceless little gnome, sprang towards him.

"Now!" shouted Toddy, and Tiny fired the giant catapult. Bags of flour rained down upon the startled fox, bursting in great white clouds. Everyone cheered and the fox ran away into the forest, never to be seen again. He had learnt his lesson; gnomes are not to be trifled with!

RAINBOW'S END